Life After Dark

(Messages of Hope)

Jessa Erandio et al

Ukiyoto Publishing

All global publishing rights are held by

Ukiyoto Publishing

Published in 2022

Contents

Introduction

Hope is everywhere. It is all around you. It thrives and it survives, no matter how dark your life has become. There is life after dark and it is hope that lives within you that keeps you alive.

Hope is never gone. You just have to open your heart and let it in.

Life After Dark (Messages of Hope) is a compilation of poetry and prose written by various writers who share the same passion about hope and life. It aims to inspire people through their words, provide encouragement and simply help anyone who feels like they are alone. This lovely little book will serve as your companion through life's ups and downs.

Poems by Ashley Oting

Hope

Standing on the last cliff

where shattered dreams and lost souls have fallen,

time moves ever so quickly

but you remain to see the world in slow motion.

and you whisper to yourself, **"What is hope, again?"**

Waiting for the last train home,

the one that leads to nowhere.

People move ever so swiftly

but you remain to move in slow motion.

and you whisper to yourself, **"Somebody, what is hope again?"**

You leave the door slightly ajar

hoping that by the time the clock strikes 12

and the grandfather clock chimes ominously,

light can enter through that small crack.

You keep whispering to yourself, **"What is hope?"**

But dear, hope hides somewhere on that last cliff

where you stood, it hangs in the balance

It is the flicker of the firefly and the gust of wind

It is heard in the crashing of the waves on the boulders.

Hope is the distant star in the horizon, ready to light your way home.

It sits next to a stranger in the last train home

It is listening to music and it remains watchful

It is listening to you and watching you

It sits there, waiting for you to look its way so it can smile at you.

It is the footsteps you hear after waiting and waiting for the light,

the gentle sun rays hitting your wooden floors

and the lamp you leave on, just in case.

Hope doesn't enter through the door slightly ajar.

It is already there in your room waiting for you to acknowledge its presence.

The songs you have on stereo, the ones you used to dance to the plant you stopped watering for how many days

the scarf your mother gave you when you celebrated your birthday.

the books written by your favorite authors.

The sound of your own heart beating and the many breaths you take.

Hope is waiting for you.

An Uninvited Guest

Pain

it comes uninvited

gripping you by the hand

choking you in your sleep

reminding you why you see only the world through a dark lens

it comes in many different faces

loss

sickness

abuse

unexplained loneliness

love

and sometimes, after *happiness*

pain

it comes *uninvited*

barging in doors with a bouquet of fresh flowers

and sometimes, we welcome it with open arms.

If on a 3 am, it comes knocking

calling for your name

in the sweetest voice,

ever dearest, *open your door wide.*

let it in.

Serve some snacks for when it sits on your living room,

sit with it.

Comfortably, listen to its stories.

When you have spent a good time with it

remind the time,

say you have another guest coming in.

tell pain that happiness will pay you a visit,

the way it did.

Pain, in the words of John Green, **demands to be felt.**

so feel it,

but never let it overstay its welcome.

Leave a room for happiness to sit, too.

Metanoia

Far ahead in the distant horizon

a rainbow awaits

as the freezing winter lingers

spring waits with the warm sun

ready to rise and bless the snow-blanketed soil

and you will for sure, see the rainbow.

As time runs its course

wounds and burns and bruises on the skin

will soon heal

however tattooed they have been

they will be there,

but believe me,

they will stop bleeding.

they will stop burning in pain

and you will for sure, be proud you have them.

The world will keep spinning

and the seasons will keep on changing

leaves will turn brown and summers will remain
scorching

flowers will bloom and wilt and the winter will keep
on biting

everything will keep moving on their own pace,

and you will for sure, keep going.

For what has been broken will soon be mended;

What has dried up will soon spring forth life;

What time ruined, it fixes.

You are worth it,

more than you could ever know.

Flow with time,

spin with mother earth,

watch the sunrise and the sunset.

Live.

Live and feel everything

as if it's the last time you ever will.

Listener

I can tell by the look in your eyes that the world has been harsh to you.

Your shoulders feel heavy and you keep dragging your feet.

Tell me what troubles you and together, we'll share that load.

I will not tell you anything.

I will just listen to you as you speak.

Nor will I judge you and tell you that you can't feel that way.

I will only listen to you.

And if you need a shoulder, I'll be close by.

You can lean on me and you can cry all you want.

Tell me what troubles you

and we'll cage them in bubbles

then send them up in the air

where they can vanish.

It will take time and they will linger up there.

They will stay there and they will keep bothering you
but at least, you got them out.

Come to me
I'll be your company.

Where Humanity Lies

You wonder how they do it;

how they smile after they make a fool out of you,

but dearly beloved,

you forget that humanity

lies not in inflicting pain;

it lies not in giving the pain back

to the people who hurt you

or to the world which knew nothing more than

to keep you on your knees.

Rather,

it lies in vulnerability.

Humanity is found in feeling the pain,

instead of giving it to others.

Humanity lies

where the clouds are always gray,

but where the sun is ever ready to keep you warm
once more.

Your pain is temporary.
Your sadness is fleeting.

So promise me,

promise me you'll keep walking with time.

Keep moving.
Keep walking.
Keep going.

Wildflower

People tend to say we always run back to what hurt us; that the comfort in familiarity is far too warm that we are afraid to take one step away from it, for the cold outside it is biting. that no matter how painful it is, we still call it part of the home we try so hard to build. And i tell you, I agree with them. Indeed, there is comfort in familiarity. Even I had a hard time letting go of the things I got so used to, you know, taking bare minimums from relationships, being treated like an option, when i know full well that I am worth choosing, feeling guilty over choosing myself, feeling guilty after asking for compromise and most of all, absorbing almost everything, even the things I know full well I can't do. *Not knowing how to say NO.*

But let this be a reminder to you, dearly beloved that indeed, it might be difficult to leave the comforts of familiarity and all, you have to understand that growth will ask so much from you. growing will need you to be out there in the freezing cold, until you build your own shelter, until you learn to thrive without the things you have become so familiar with. ***Even if there is comfort in familiarity, remember that peace and freedom wait for you outside of that box you willingly lock yourself in.***

So, grow. Leave that cramped up space and grow.

Learn to say NO. Set your boundaries. Don't ever get used to being in pain. Refuse to take the bare minimum because you know you deserve more than that. You don't have to lower your standard just so they could reach you. You don't need to feel guilty for choosing your peace. Remember that when you grow, you become a bigger person. You will take up space and that is **alright.** Let go of that familiar warmth you keep coming home to, because let me be brutally honest. **It is not helping you grow.** It is hindering your growth. You will be like a wildflower planted in a small pot. You will not grow into your full potential.

The pain you willingly eat every meal, the pain you think you deserve keeps you there. So, let it all go. Be kind to yourself. Refuse to take that pain anymore. You have suffered enough. You have done enough. Let it all go. Leave.

Remember, dearly beloved. Let things go. Step out into the open and see where all these struggles take you. I assure you. the world will hurt you, it surely will. But what it gives, it heals. What it inflicts, it sends you healing in many forms. people. pets. books. small gestures. kind words. You will find it. You will find it anywhere.

Grow. Take up space. Bloom into the wildflower that you are.

Be Gentle With Yourself

Be gentle with yourself.

Be gentle with yourself on days when you want push back the plate and just watch your food go cold, unmoved, and uneaten.

Be gentle with yourself on days when you can't look at yourself in the mirror, because your pimples have left ugly blotches on your cheeks. Pinkish and hideous.

Be gentle with yourself on days when you refuse to take a shower or even wash your hands.

Be gentle with yourself on days when you feel like you are the ugliest person in the middle of a crowded room, with people full of fake smiles living almost-perfect lives. (*nothing is as it seems.*)

Be gentle with yourself on days when you refuse to sleep just to watch the moon hide behind gray clouds and be eaten by the sun when the dusk comes.

Be gentle with yourself when you see your scars bleed on the inside. Your wounds need tender loving care.

Be very gentle with yourself on days you think you can't get anything right. You are trying to find the right footing.

Be very gentle with yourself on your darkest days.

You need it more than the days you feel beautiful and glowing.

Be very gentle with yourself.

You are doing great, and I am proud of you.

The Little Things

Go.

Go make that cup of coffee

And sip it like it will be your last.

Go for a drive and park by the seashore,

Or anywhere overlooking the horizon

Where the sky meets the sea.

Perhaps, watch the kids run on the pathway next to your house,

While you chew the burnt cookie you baked early in the morning.

Pretend that you added dark chocolate chip cookies in the batter.

Savor the bitterness, eat it like it will be the last time you will eat one.

Exist like today is the last.

Do it every day.

Find beauty in the simple things.

Make it worth doing.

You have to find joy in these little things,

Make them count like the big things too.

From the smell of the roasted coffee

To the smell of the rain on the pavement

Or the smell of the pages of your books.

You have to find it.

It is all around you.

Hold on to it.

Make everything worth doing.

Forgiveness

For all those nights you sat in your bed

watching the night sky turn to blood red,

those days you had to put on a brave face

and go on with your usual routine unfazed.

For all those times you held back your tears

while you watch all of them come to life and chase
you, your fears

those times all you did was remember

how once in your life, that night in September

all you had ever known was happiness in shades of
blue

and everything you had to do was be free and true.

Did you forgive yourself?

For all those nights you had to whisper to yourself
that your only company will be grief
those times you cannot complete the puzzle
and you just break down and watch the rain trickle,
for all those nights you felt left out
while all the world moved about
forward and brave
while you are there, stuck and dazed.

For refusing to be hugged warmly
but yearning to be cared for ever so truly
for pushing people away
but longing for them to look away.

Did you forgive yourself?

But dearly beloved, remember the times you stood up / wiped your tears and put your make up on / the times you sang songs in the shower / dancing around the kitchen while you make yourself a hearty meal after brawling with an exhausting breakdown / remember the times you went out / danced under the pouring rain / letting the cool raindrops bless you with its freeing sensation while the sun shone so brightly / the times you watched how the different seasons have turned / from the blooming of flowers to the browning of leaves / to the melting of snowflakes on the tip of your nose and the scorching beach days / the sound of the winds rustling / brushing against each other / and your hands on the dusty piano keys / playing major keys and happy melodies.

REMEMBER IT ALL.

Will you forgive yourself?

(*It has to start with you.*)

Adam

Dearly beloved,

Endless summers will burn your skin,

and bone-chilling winters will freeze your heart.

The dead leaves will remind you so much of the many times you have been on the inside

and the spring will no longer be as vibrant as it did before to you.

But remember that beauty is present in the brown-orange pigment of leaves,

and the way they sway in the air as they fall to the ground will remind you

to take your steps slowly and surely.

Remember that new beginnings are found in the blooming of flowers;

and the first drop of soft rain.

It is found in the first drop of a cute snowflake on the tip of your nose

and the way it melts.

New beginnings spring forth with the new leaves coming from a dry tree after the fall,

and it is found under the scorching heat of the sun.

Keep your head up.

New beginnings come.

and bad days don't last.

Poems by Bon Ramniel Morales

Into the Storm

Winds are howling, the skies are crying,
And there you are, watching, pretending to hear
nothing but silence,
It's better than a pointless shouting,
Still voiceless even though you gave everything.

Surrounded by hundreds of cyclones
But dare to tell no one,
A rampaging scream inside your bones,
Yet again, you tell not a single soul.

Maybe, just maybe the darkness of the sky is
comforting,
You can manage to hide all of those messy feelings
Lonely but not alone,
Like the eye of a typhoon.

Into the eye of the storm
There was you hoping for a dawn,
For a calming daylight and for you to continue to
fight for life,
You need to survive, you need to be alive.

Happier than Ever

After the storm, a ball of sunshine will rise,
Warm breeze will hug us tight,
To ease away the pain, to give us holy light
And most importantly, to heal these wounds of ours
that cannot be seen by the naked sight.

After the earthquake, everything will be calm
When it stop shaking, humans will be humans,
Plants will grow green and we'll have bountiful
number of animals,
Our land, is our land.

We'll have a better place
Even if everything is still a mess,
We will rise again,
And be happier than ever.

Cry Trying

Light up the sky,
You need to let it all go tonight
For you have been driven tired,
Wanting to quit lying in silence
You don't want to live this way,
Because everyday you feel insane,
Crying for better days—
So keep on trying,
Even if it means falling.

Life in the Dark

Buried six feet underground, you died.
Breathing was never an option, I know you tried.
It was freezing dark and you're naked, surrounded
with shadows full of hatred—
you cursed, shouted, and lost it,
Wanted to forget, but still, wanna breathe.

Life in the dark, grasping for a beam of light
A small amount will keep you going through,
To wash away the hate,
to move on and never lose faith.

To trust you, yourself again.

Your Truth

Open your eyes and face your hideous self
Let your veins be run through with guilt,
Clean up the mess that you've made,
It's okay to be wrong but please admit your mistakes.

We all have dark and uncolored sides,
Life in the dark made us feel that bad is right
But, *with a little touch of light,*
Change, *change is not that bad.*

***There are mirrors of truth and there are
reflections of lies,***
It is up for us to decide:
Where to look to and where to smile,
One glance is equal to one truth and twice a stare
gives bountiful lies.

No matter what the shape of glass is like,
You are ugly, said by your lie.

Believe

When you believed, you believed
But until when?
Of course forever, even if you know you can't.

Go as far as you can, conquer the world with the
power of courage
You are never just a person,
You can cross every bridge

Just believe in yourself,
You are more than anything.

Someone

Became someone, you never knew
Everything's so new,
Is it really you?
You still don't know what to do
Sick of asking things out of the blue
You didn't lose people, they lost you,
Actually no...
You lost yourself in loving someone who only sees the good in you.

Dream

As long as you wake up everyday,
No one can take your dreams away
Believe, that's what you've been telling yourself,
So do as your soul said;
Trust the process,
Your sweat and tears will lead to success.

Dreams are meant to be inspirations,
Don't let them fade away with their high expectations,
It is you who's responsible,
It is up to you to decide what's possible and
impossible,
It is your life, it is your choice,
Keep on dreaming, be your own voice.

Faking It

You're still there, cherishing those memories,
Not getting tired of turning every damn pages
I know you want to forget, but how, when they
already marked your lips?
Now all you're looking for is that poisonous kiss.

Her photo on your wallet,
With your anniversary written on it,
You didn't throw it away on purpose,
And indeed that was a fake reason.

You can't, with your smiling faces
Fooling you away, losing every chances,
You manage to stay in the dark,
But it's time to move on and tear that photo

Hoping the day would come, the day that you could
say it's just another picture to burn,

No hesitations, no return
Don't want any wrong turn,

But again, that's just another fake reason.

Ready to Go

Black footsteps of yesterday,
Followed by a fresh heartbreak,
You are broken and unfixed, doesn't have a reason to
stay,
But you stand still,
Waiting for that wounds of promises to heal,
Despite of being cracked, you smile like nothing
happened, you are so well...

in hiding pain.

You are ready to go,
To put on a fantastic show
Because even though
You are filled with storm,
Nothing good will come out if sadness is born
So you choose to let go instead of holding onto those
messy emotions.

You are strong,
So *you smiled at the eye of the storm.*

Poems by Jhannah Paguyo

Daggers of Hope

You gave your sorrows a home, that it embraced your insides and ate you whole.

You asked yourself a hundred of times

"Where did it go wrong? Why can't you find peace?"

It was an unanswered prayer, a whisper of the cold wind, no one listens to your pleas.

A childhood that was destroyed, snatched, and damaged.

You are lost to find the path that you will take, it is hard and you can't choose the right image.

You are stuck in a random black whole – paralyzed and immovable.

There is no mark of bliss.

It was full of twist and turn.

But then, there are daggers of hope.

You will burn but you will rise and try.

So, let your wings fly and reach for the sky.

Along with the arrival of twilight is your sailing in darkness.

Silhouette of Grief

Whisper of despair

A cycle that is beyond repair.

Shadows of sorrow in a sleepless silence long,

This lifetime is teasing you so hard that you can't stand strong.

If only you knew that his time would be short, you would have spent every rides with him.

You won't sing shadows of regrets in dim.

If only you knew that this lifetime was fast.

You would have enjoyed the mesmerizing sunrise until it last.

You crave for a warmth hug from above, to put an end to a non-stop flash of regrets.

To embrace the light silhouette.

You can now, stop living an extra heart for someone.

You can have it your way,

As they save you an empty seat in paradise.

Death is inevitable – it will knock on one's door to rip one's soul.

Stop living in grief now, the one thing you can do is to treasure the moments.

Remember that tomorrow is never promised.

So, cherish memories today, because yesterday is gone in the winds.

The sands of time are bursting.

The future is unknown –

Life is just burrowing of bones.

Fleeting Love

The memories are flashing back to you–

Like a haunting ghost and a fleeting embrace of the tormenting past.

You want these recollections to vanish in the vast thin air.

You gave your farewell a long time ago,

But it still lingers in your soul.

It's a trauma of a first love.

The one that has not got away because it is a battle that was never fought for.

A love that was sweet but short-lived.

It was an unexpected falling,

Fast beating, surely, but heart-wrecking.

It was a love in the dark.

A not so perfect love, at a wrong time.

First love, frequently persist in one's heart –

Just like fireworks, it was a love that light up beautifully.

It was short, that you saw it with your own two eyes – it disappeared in the cold dark sky.

As the wind kiss your skin, you know it's time to set yourself free from that darkness.

Unleashing Love

As the wind blows your silky long hair.

You breathe the freezing summer air.

Decades have past, yet you are still here.

Silently, longing for a love that results in silent madness.

It only results in a hollow on your chest.

A love that burns, the one that cuts you too.

Under iridescent skies, life threw you to the raging waves.

You aren't a swimmer, **but this love drowned you beneath.**

You gasp for salt air, until it fills your lungs.

Life gave you a piece of heaven and an entirety of hell.

But, never again will you fight for a love that can cause you a lifetime to be reciprocated.

Never again will you taste a glimpse of bare minimum.

You are tough just like your decisions,

Despite of what if's of holding on or letting go.

You'll let go of a love that does not help you grow.

Leave that love from the dark.

To free a love even you are holding it without hands.

It's time to rise in a garden of doomed.

Right now, you'll choose to love you.

Until you're whole and a day will come, **the "right love" will find "you."**

One's Sanctuary

In just a simple act of kindness

In death, someone can be saved...

You can only hope to keep going,

But it seems like all roads in your life that you take, are always running at a dead end.

You took a glimpse of an empty life, and a faceless future.

A shadow that one cannot see, life's torture.

There are nights when painful memories flow endlessly.

No matter how much you sail, your thoughts still sink you.

In the depths of blue,

You surf the dark wave's monstrosity.

Nevertheless, *there is a warm embrace in the dark, shivering, cold wind.*

A mellow music in a shrill melody.

A beacon of hope, the peace in chaos, and a hand to hold.

The bursting sun rays whenever your world is pulled by darkness.

A shoulder to cry on when you are chased by sadness.

The soul that knows that there is fury in your every laugh.

A touch of solicitude in your lost soul.

Trials are beyond the numbers of twinkling stars.

But there are a hundred ways, to start again.

A hundred reasons to live again.

New beginnings - a clean state.

You are destined to continue, you are bound to fight

Against the whips of burning fire and blow of raging seas.

The dullness shall pass and you will find your flickering light.

Lonely Young Shoulders

Loneliness embrace your soul that you got used to it.

You just let it go, rent for free that it feels familiar and comfortable.

It became thicker, your shoulder's baggage is heavier.

You gave it a home, that it visits you every now and then.

The darkness consumed you, it peels your skin off until you're undressed and naked.

Letting the gloomy day stay, like an old and broken radio playing repeatedly.

It is a monotonous routine –

It is tiring and wears you down.

Nevertheless, despite of loneliness,

Hope will wave at you at the horizon,

Along with its vibrant colors, you won't feel alone.

So now, *step forward without glancing back from the door of misery.*

Please stop carrying the guilt they gave you.

You have done your part a long time ago.

It is a pain on your young shoulders.

Ain't feeble soul.

Life's Comma

For the past years, you've been stuck in the darkness.

The dreadful bile in your throat.

You've been busy, have a hectic schedule.

You've been grinding half of your life that you forgot how to enjoy.

You forgot how it feels to be appreciative, to glance all the places you've been through.

Maybe for a moment, you took a glimpse of it.

But truth to be told, you never had a chance to adore it completely.

Because you've been hustling until you run dry and cold.

You've achieved so much, but you aren't happy.

You've grind most of your life yet never at peace and contented.

You are on the top, as high as skyscrapers.

But no one taught you that **"the brighter the light on you, the darker the shadow."**

But now, you can pause for a while.

Try to see a glimpse of scenery that you've forgotten a long time ago.

You can now rest and breathe.

You've been in the dark for too long.

It's Cloudy Outside

They said it is raining today, but I know it's been raining most of your life.

The life you've encountered wasn't easy,

It's like a two-edged sword ready to rip you apart.

It's a gloomy feeling, a hurricane in your insides.

You stumble and fall – you even lost your pride.

The journey you've been through was not rainbows and butterflies.

At a midpoint, you lost yourself...

You even think of suicide.

But today, it is cloudy outside.

It is time to go, let the rain go away.

Now, you must let go of the excruciating pain.

As the shadows of red and orange are arising.

The hue from above is waving and you will rise up too.

Bloom in Time

A lost flower in the dark and empty horizon.

Along with those burdens, you chose to build a garden.

Flowers pick, you thought they will help you grow, instead they cut you deep.

Like a shallow water with six feet depth.

They left you with flowers dry and lifeless butterflies;

With broken memories and unsaid goodbyes,

What if's which can no longer speak.

Empty promises of an abundant life.

Regardless of loneliness, you prefer to bloom.

Progressively, surely you will rise in the abyss of gloom.

You bequeathed the storms.

Now, continue to survive.

With shattered pieces, continue to stand firm.

You will bloom in time...

Slowly but beautifully.

Poems by Judy Azul

Sunset

If the sunset's hue

makes you feel blue,

Change the way you view

It can make you feel happy too.

Self-Respect

Sometimes, you have to give up loving
someone to gain self-respect,
and you should stop tolerating bad things
and words that you don't deserve.

Plans

If things don't work according to your plans,

Maybe it's not meant to be yours.

But for sure, behind it, there's a purpose.

It may come in the form of a blessing in disguise,

Because His plans are always better than ours.

Be Kind

Each day is an opportunity for you to be happy.
Try to smile even if you're in the middle of uncertainties.
Be kind to yourself.

Rain

The rhythm of the rain
reminds you of the pain.
It keeps pouring and makes
you feel like mourning.

But you still can keep soaring,
Don't let it keep you in vain.
Now, please stop worrying.
Soon you will be happy again.

Enough Is Enough

Some people will hate you or treat you as invisible

But **the best thing about pain is that you will learn**

and grow from all the heartaches you passed.

Being alone will give you more time to work on yourself

and find true happiness.

Letting go of all the ones who hurt you will change your life.

When enough is enough, don't let them act too much.

Overseas

You've been away for so many years,
Letting yourself sleep at night with tears.
Longing for hugs from a family that cares,
Missing their love that no one compares.

For now, you might be oceans apart,
But soon, you'll be home and won't depart.
Happiness will fulfill your aching heart,
And you can have a brand new start.

You can spend more quality time,
Whether it rains or shines.

Never Too Late

It's never too late to say "I'm sorry"
to the people you did betray.
It's never too late to kneel down and pray.
It's never too late to ask forgiveness out of dismay.
It's never too late to save yourself from agony.

Let Go

Do you know why it's hard to be happy?
Because we refuse to let go
of the situations that make us sad.

Let go if you have to.
Do not compromise your happiness
over nonsensical things.

Breadwinner

A title that you didn't choose,
And neither you can refuse.
Breadwinner, it sounds cool,
Others treat you as their idol.

Due dates here, duties there
Bills are waiting everywhere.
It's on your list- you are aware,
though you feel it's a bit unfair.

Have a lot of mouths to feed,
Lending the things they need.
Soon, all of you will succeed,
You will reap what you planted.

Though you have lots of complaints,
You still choose to be patient.
You do a job well done in your role,
And slowly fulfilling your goal.

Poems by Jessa Erandio

If Hope Has A Name

Does hope really die? When you have nothing left, does hope leave you too? Probably not, for **hope is a life constant**. It is always within yourself.

Hope, it's just a four-letter word but it could have a million different meanings. *Hope is the joy* you feel when flowers are in bloom during winters or when crops become abundant after being in drought. *Hope is the excitement* you feel after passing an exam that you've been trying to pass for a couple of times already. *Hope is the love* you feel for the first time again, after being heartbroken for so many times. *Hope is the passion* you feel for something again when it seems like you've lost everything, *Hope is the strength* you feel after being weakened by life's challenges.

Hope is the last train you caught that took you to your destination. Hope is the light at the end of the tunnel. Hope is giving birth after many miscarriages. Hope is recovering from a fatal accident or a life-threatening ailment. Hope is standing again after falling down badly. Hope is being resilient after every devastation, after every storm, after every unwanted situation.

Hope is the thing that keeps you alive. It exists because something existed before and that's the best thing about hope. It comes out not when times are easy but when times are tough. You may fall so many times but it's hope that will make you rise. True enough, **if hope has a name, it would be --- EVERYTHING.**

Beauty in Bravery

There is beauty in bravery,
when you are able to fight
with all your might
to *give yourself some liberty.*

There is beauty in bravery,
when you don't easily give up
although challenges don't stop
crushing your soul constantly.

There is beauty in bravery
but it's often replaced by fears,
worries, anxieties and tears,
that seem to ruin your life completely.

There is beauty in bravery,
when you face life head on
with resilience and hope as your weapon
to survive life victoriously

One Day

One day,
the world will be
a better place to live in.

One day,
you will be free
from something that cages you.

One day,
your life will change
and you'll know it's for the best.

Until the day comes,
live as if every day is your last
and embrace every change
no matter how big or small it is.

Constant Sunshine

Sometimes, darkness surrounds your whole being. It's like whatever you do, negativities are all around you. You work hard, you get useless. You give your all, still it is not enough. Not everything goes out as you planned. You love someone so much, but you are not loved back.

Nonetheless, you should realize that life is just as it is. Living life is really not that easy because if it is just easy, you wouldn't value it that much. Every single person and circumstance in your life is indispensable. You learn something from them and in one way or another, they leave a mark in your life that will always be in your memory.

So, *even if life gets really dark, find your constant sunshine.* It can be a loved one, your family, your friends, or even, your own self. **Sometimes, you don't need anyone to light up your life because there's a light in you that comes from within.**

Wanderer

You are just a wanderer
cruising through tides of time
Live, as you wish,
put all your past behind.
Live in the moment,
but still think about the future.

In this transient life,
if you won't go with the flow,
you will never be able to grow.

The Right Perspective

Life sometimes pushes you hard
with all the stress and the challenges.
You get busy with your everyday endeavor.
Sometimes, you get sick and fall down.

Many times, you had to decide
what is right from what is wrong.
No matter what situation you're in,
if you're brave enough to fight,
you'll be strong enough to survive.
It's just a matter of having the right perspective.

Rain of Hope

Hope pours when you need it the most
When you're feeling alone and lost,
When you're looking for something to hold on to,
Hope comes, to bring your faith anew

For a farmer, the pour of the rain is hope
For a driver, a safe travel is hope
For a teacher, a new student is hope
For a writer, a finished piece is hope

Whenever you think that hope is gone,
Think again, for hope always comes
It's like a gift you receive unexpectedly
That will turn your life around completely.

Heart Glows In The Dark

Though your soul is slipping away,

your faith is diminishing everyday,

you're losing your cherished sanity,

and your light is fading slowly,

don't ever let go of the spark

for **your heart glows in the dark.**

You just have to fight until the very end

And *don't let the chaos make you bend*

Symphony of Poetry

Does ache lock the secrets to becoming happy? The more pain you endure, does that mean it's the happier you will be?

If there's one thing that everyone has experienced at least once, it's being in pain. Pain comes in different forms but they are all the same in causing misery and loneliness. Not to romanticize solitude and pain but there's something about being in this state that makes people more alive.

Some people may have already thought, "If my tears turn into pearls, I'll be the wealthiest person on Earth" and so they let their tears flow naturally, without holding back. They simply love the idea that pain, after all, is what makes people appreciate life.

And this very idea gave birth to poetry. Pain created the best poets who ever lived. Melancholy is the driving force behind people who got lost and found in poetry.

Have you ever tried writing your heart out? Regardless of the emotions you are feeling, write about it. You can use poetry as a form of catharsis for the things you wanted to say but couldn't convey. Delve into the realm of poetry and have the chance to make your melancholy, something that is worth remembering and writing about. In people's esoteric eyes, your feelings may not be valid, but still, write about it. No matter how dark your thoughts may be, they are still a part of you, so you should embrace them. You cannot be whole without the dark but you should never let it consume you. Instead, use the dark as inspiration and your light within will emerge.

So, the next time you feel like you're drowning from pain and anxiety, get your pen and paper and start writing. It may not solve all of your problems but it will allow you to handle them better by having an avenue to release them.

Let your words flow with your ocean of emotions.

Let your mind and soul free.

Let yourself be saved by poetry.

Your Life Purpose

Who and what do you wake up for?

Sometimes, life gets too busy or messed up that you don't really know what's going on. You bombard yourself with too many questions that in the end are left unanswered. With everything that's been happening, *you forget things that are more important* like spending time with your loved ones, pampering yourself and keeping close communication with others.

You may not always know what your purpose in life is yet, but you have a whole lifetime to figure it all out.

Poems by Danna Garbida

Cope With Hope

Who taps your back, in the toughness of life

To hold your palm, to cheer you up?

Who got your back when life seems dark

To hold your arm. to check you up?

You'll know that **to cope with hope, is to still find hope.**

Searching, no one to go. Believe, you'll alone grow.

You have all the process, you can soon walk into the glow

From all the dark steps, challenge again your life test.

You've made it all the way to survive,

You've got it with hope, you can still give it a try.

You can all do things, there is God as your guide.

You can survive, again, again and again - not only a trice.

It's not easy to say, you can't do it every time.

Sometimes it just happens out of nowhere.

You'll not trust it and still have to deal with it.

Life is tough and you are too.

The Best Is Yet To Come

The best is yet to come, as you walk out of the darkness

As you lit up your candles, you'll soon find hope.

Amidst you falling back to life, as you think you can't walk out.

Even your light wasn't enough to still hold on and still find hope.

You can slow down, take and still

a little by little step.

You have all the moments to believe.

If it's helping you from time to time-

You can standby and wait,

It's still gonna happen, the best is yet to come.

Amal is Hope

Everything is gonna be exhausting.
One day you'll find waking up in the morning,
Is something exciting
You'll breathe and sip your coffee
You'll see sunshine and lend a smile.

Everything is gonna be exhausting.
One night you'll hide your lights
Take a step to hide in the dark,
Will not breathe for a moment.

Everything is gonna be exhausting,
Every day is gonna be a battle.
Sometimes you'll win,
Sometimes you'll lose.

You'll still gonna find amal
From everything exhausting
You'll still see light.
Every morning and night.

Hope in the Quiet

They say, serenity at its finest.
There is hope in the stillness.
While you breathe slowly.
To silence your mind - if only.

The rhythm of this poetry
Can crank all your words.
Making an outcry to your thoughts.
Invading your silence in the darkness.

No more painstaking words.
Poems can light up your torch.
And take all your worries in life.
You'll make it this time.

Let all the rhythm,
No more silence.
Hope in the quiet.
You can make it.

"Hope Matters"

Has it ever happened to you?

You, staring at yourself in the mirror asking what you have done to your life

Fighting back your tears from falling,

Cuz, everything did not happen according to its place.

Thinking how you could take all the broken things back to their destined pieces.

No one to talk to, and more doubts as you walk.

Silent in every step yet thoughts are running away.

Don't wanna make a drama in life, just wanna hold a knife.

Not to kill yourself, but to kill the monsters- your thoughts.

Yet, you staring at yourself in the mirror asking what you have done to your life.

Then, you still got many things to do,

Paper works to finish and documents to compile.

Clothes to clutter and errands to do.

That is what you think you must do,

Yet, no motivation to start.

Hey! Hope got your back!

It may not matter all day and night.

It happens not just by chance.

It's already part of life.

A minute it can banish,

A second it comes back,

You may not notice it - it's like magic.

Like a candle that eats the dark.

Hope is like that,

That's why it matters in life.

Before you end this line.

Think about if it matters.

Have a second thought about it.

Poetry is Hope

Rhymes playing in your ears

While you let fall, your tears

Poems are how you find hope.

When life tries you to cope.

You can't alone take this risk

Hope without poetry, is hope without e

You'll just hop in fear.

Lonely dear, no one will hear.

Poetry is hope, this craft is not a joke.

It's deadly serious, it can save your soul.

Powerful than what you think it is.

Words can breathe and run through your blood.

You just have to hold on a little longer.

For it's not easy, there is no such thing as speed recovery.

You can still believe, that poetry is hope.

Take all the rhythm and read this as a song.

Life After Dark

Life after dark, you think it's gonna be the same again?

That all that you got, is gonna vanish in disdain

All the hustle of surviving will go back in pain

Oh, no, you gotta be kidding, cuz it ain't gonna happen.

It's gonna change, a huge bucket of change.

Like it's a process of euphoria, purring all over

It will give rise next chapter, not the final episode

It's gonna be you again and it's gonna be bolder.

You are not the same character, you did grow

You can take all the worries and you are still fighting

You'll have more doubts and think all night in a row

It's fine and normal, it's hard for your tired soul - not a bad thing.

Take the moment of this uncomfortable feeling

It's happening for a reason, every season

You've lost people and memories all the way

You did things you thought you can't - you're a brave soul.

Hold on a little lighter, there is still sunshine and moonlight

It's happening every day and night, so thus you must do it.

You've come way too far to travel and take this craft.

You know you can do it and yes you are - you're a brave soul.

You're a new person now, you should be proud

Tiniest Sign of Light

You'll find comfort in the cold.

With the breeze, you'll still breathe

You'll stay longer in the dark.

That illuminates the tiniest sign of light.

It's okay, it's valid, you can stay in silence

You can't always be tough and fake a laugh.

Sometimes that is what life needs - to pause.

When you're feeling lost.

Yet, at the moment, you can look back.

Appreciate why you did start.

Heartbreak can't wholly crush your soul.

You'll get up and grow soon.

Even all that you got is the tiniest sign of light.

It's still a symbol of hope, amidst the cold.

It may not warm you for good.

You know it's something hopeful to feel and see.

In The Darkness, You Will Never Hide.

Gone is the darkness, you had surpassed
From all night, of no light.
You're not alone, don't hide.
You can't die without this line.

Poetry got your back
From the rhythm and verses
From all the lines and stanzas
Find its hidden meaning - its art

You'll remember this part,
Take a moment to start.
Save this poem for life.
In the darkness, you will never hide.

Not again, brave soul
You've done enough.
All the risks and still have doubts
You'll be saved by this craft.

Not a promise, but an assurance

It's still up to you and only about you.

Then, choose if it's flight or fight

If this light in the dark is right.

You're Here

How many times you have thought
You can't?
Yet, you are still here.
Having all the worries in life
Taking all the pills, all night.
Heavenly breathing, exhausted.

How many times you have thought
You can't?
Yet, you are still here.
Believing you'll make it again
Fighting back all doubts and pain.
Poetry is what you think will save.

How many times you have thought
You can't?
Yet, you are still here.

Now, time to light up.

Shine and spark.

Free from darkness,

No more doubts.

Stories by Angelo Estudillo

Unwritten

They believe your life has always **been** an open book, but they have no idea that this has not always been the case. You were asked a few weeks ago if you were guilty of living a double life and if you were attempting to make a better impression of yourself rather than being genuine to yourself. You've been pondering that subject for quite some time. It's not that you've lived in deception or been untruthful; rather, *you've been so protective of yourself from pain and grief* that only people you trust have access to the pages of your existence. Your experiences had left you with little choice but to construct your barriers and refuse to allow anyone into your world. "In that way, you were being honest with yourself and not pretending to be someone you are not." Maybe. You guess so. **Your past will always be a part of you**, but it will not define how you live in the present or in the future. Your life is a never-ending story full of ups and downs, twists, and turns. Your book's unseen and untold stories are still alive and well. The Master Writer is still working on some pages.

There were pages ripped and burned, never to be seen again. Nobody can live your story or determine how it will end. Many critics will attempt to criticize and critique your book just based on its cover, without reading the narratives. They only select what they wish to read rather than reading it in its entirety. They got to the end of your story without getting to the core of it. They only judge your book on the outside. Many people will come and go in your lifetime and will try to create their own plot of your story. **They will rip out the pages of what they think is right or wrong, trying to leave their marks in your book.** They can try but they can never take away your choice to lead your life the Master Writer wants it to. *These pages of your book carries hope.*

Bathos

Sinking deep,
gasping for air
Sinking deep,
humid nightmare
Sinking deep,
into vast emptiness
Sinking deep,
faded memories,
motionless,
drowning,
plunging,
into weariness
Sinking deep,
into rejections
Sinking deep,
unmet expectations
Sinking deep,
out of breath
Sinking deep,
into death.

The heavens

must have heard
never have forgotten
rescued by His word

Waking up,
seeing the light
Waking up,
day is bright
Waking up,
renewed vision
Waking up,
moving on
breathing,
living,
Waking up,
from gloom
Waking up,
You have hope
You are home.

Into The Realm of Butterflies

A streak of light
An immovable train
How was your flight?
Do you also feel pain?

Slowly waking up from slumber
You envy their secret bond to flowers
Breaking from fantasy chamber
Are your chances outnumbered?

Have you ever had a broken wing?
For a hundred times, you were held by a string.
If they could break free from their chrysalis,
then you can also from your stygian darkness.

Sonnet VI

When the lullaby of spring lingers on

that deep chasm is flooded with dejection
you sigh for the things forgotten and mourn
and remember her as your companion
then those yearning be filled with overflow.
The train of life goes with melancholy
But does it only traverse sorrow?
or does **life have its** moments of glory?
Then when her lullabies flood your damn soul
The weight of the heavy burden is lifted.
Her lullabies filled your head to sole.
Will her songs to the afterlife be carried?

As long as the train of life progresses
Her lullabies will give your life essence

Towards The Light

Let the chasm descend upon us,
and all we have is indignation
to keep us from stumbling.
A dying rose
in the window pane
facing the light,
a golden spirit,
our time has come;
the shadow disappears.

Paradox

And in the shadow of the day, hope lies

And in the lowtides of the heart, life exists

And in the stench of death, eternal life begins

Rumor of a World Without Tears

There is a rumor of a city made of precious stones and minerals wherein the wall was made of jasper, and the city of pure gold, as pure as glass. The foundations of the city walls were decorated with every kind of precious stone. The gates were made of pearls. The "Master" of this City once said "Do not let your hearts be troubled. Trust my Father and trust me also. In my Father's house are many rooms; if it were not so, I would have told you. I am going there to prepare a place for you. And if I go and prepare a place for you, I will come back and take you to be with me that you also may be where I am."

There is hope knowing one day, the "Master" will return. You will no longer shed tears in that city He is preparing. I know this for sure because not only He said He is going to prepare a place for you and me but He also said, "I will wipe away every tear from their eyes, and death shall be no more, neither shall there be mourning, nor crying, nor pain anymore, for the former things have passed away. I am making things new."

The Rumor of A World Without Tears will remain a rumor for those who refuse to repent and believe in the Master's return. For now, you hold on, grow your faith, and persevere. One day, you will be in paradise.

Enchanted

Paint the pulchritudinous sky
with one idiosyncratic smile
Allow it to flood your emptiness
to break the walls of darkness
and have meaningful memories

Carry On, My Friend

How are you responding
to the weight of the pandemic?
maybe this is just hard to carry
maybe you are frantic with worry
maybe afraid and hiding in the attic
anxious of the future---blurry
the days may seem long & dreary
but there is a good story
Hope is still beaming with glory.

You Are a Champion

you are feeble
so please stop persuading yourself that
you have a heart of steel
because no matter what happens
you despise every part of yourself
and you are not going to deceive yourself by stating
there is beauty in your inner strength that matters
so do not worry, please remind yourself
that you are a castle with a fragile foundation
and nothing that they speak will make you accept
you are a champion who can run the extra mile
because, regardless of the circumstances
all your efforts isn't enough to make you a Champion
and you have no reason to think that
you have inner strength within

(Please read from bottom to top)

Hope In The Rain

The sky weeps,

flooding the deep

cradled in tears

He slumbers

numb by pain,

Hope in the rain.

Dawn

Evanescent break of day,
will you linger a little longer?
You fill my life with wonder
You took away all my gray

The Antidote For Anxiety

The only cure for anxiety

is the hope of certainty

that you and the Almighty

will eventually meet one day

in a brand-new way.

Burning

Life is an uphill climb.
There are those days
you just want to give up.
There are those moments
that you get tired
going through the motion.
There are those days
days of uncertainty
when the sun
no longer shine.
You are surrounded
by toxic people,
those with the intention
to pull you down,
to make you anxious,
to wound your soul,
but they
won't succeed.
They can try,
they can try
but

you will be strong.
You will be brave.
You will keep climbing.
You will be moving on.
Will you let His light
penetrate your darkest days?
Keep your heart fully alive
until you are consumed
by this unquenchable

flame of **hope.**
You'll keep
burning!
burning!
burning!

When Darkness Draw Near

When darkness draw near,
when the path seems unclear,
when you feel low and beaten,
when you are caught in between,
would you promise to persevere
even if you badly want to surrender?
Would you choose to live fully
even if darkness draws near swiftly?

Poems by Noemi Bucasas

Play

It may always seem that the world is unkind

Whether you were born with a silver spoon in your mouth

Or born in a lowly state, as humble as a mouse

Each of us has our own story

Each of us has a burden to carry

Nevertheless, *forward is always the way to go*

Even when at times, the dark has won over our soul

Kindness is born deep within

It is for you to share and to give to one another as freely as it seems

When it feels that no one cares

There will always be a light deep in your soul

That no darkness can ever take away

Your place in this life has been marked

And you have a significant role to play…

Miracles

Look not into the sky and cry in despair

For miracles, big or small, are always sent your way

For you lived through life as if it is not fair

But look around for little blessings

Little miracles disguised as nothings

Remember that no one is insignificant

No matter how cursed your life has been…

Little blessings come in the form of every mornings,

That you wake up and still able to live the day casually;

In the form of essentials like the air we breathe,

The sunshine that beams and the rain that refreshes,

And the wind that caresses; such are nature's life bonuses-

To live and walk this earth is truly a luxury…

Family and friends, no matter how few or how many

Or how far apart, are always sent your way

To spice up your life, no matter how mundane.
Little blessings are disguised as nothings
So train your eyes to see and your heart to feel
To *make little blessings big miracles*
That you have prayed for in times of need

Hope

Hope is a light that slips out from within

When the soul is buried deep in pain and in agony

The loss of a loved one to another

The loss of a family member

Even lost opportunity or anything that matters

Hope finds you when you can no longer stand

To help you up and rebuild oneself again

When you are down on your knees

Begging and crying for the cup of life to be removed

Hope comes sweeping down to help you up

And leaves you feeling refreshed, renewed.

Life

The task is just as simple and true

To live long enough to see the morning anew

Each day springs forth a new beginning

Even if the in between are sour and bitter

Let it sleep with a happy ending altogether

Rest dear soul, do not be stressed and worried

Erase that frown of worry and remove the shroud of doubt

No better way to end all strife than to give a genuine smile

With a wink of an eye, tell life:

You always got me everytime.

Revive

Let hope take you where you belong

Love may not see you for who you really are

It takes courage to act on it

And more often than not, courage fails

Faith crumbles at a slight tremor

A glitch that can turn one's journey difficult

Making your road rough that it will tear you apart;

But ***hope gives you the light, when no other light shines***

It comes through even at that desperate moment

It revives love and faith to endure

And keeps your spirit burning with fervor at the end

Hope may see you as fragile as you are

But never fear for it will carry you far

It drives you like the wind to reach for your dreams

And will make everything right

Stitching up all ripped seams, even the heart

Carved

My life built on empty halls and cinnamon shadows
Blurry lines drawn against the rubbles
Searching for a glimmer of hope in a lost flower
Somewhere, there is something out there
Specially made for you and me
A special life carved out the palm of my hands
Life well lived with family and friends
Not too much but hoping not too less
Always, there is a spare nevertheless.
Though the eyes can be deceived
And dreams seemed to be missing from me
Along this lonely road, rocks and dirt that we tread on
No resting place for a weary traveler
And death seems to be always around the corner
Follow the unwinding path as time wore on
Different burdens to carry as the journey go on

With little strength to move along this life
Here is wishing that our light can endure

So as to life carved out our names

In the epitaph of its earth

In remembrance of how we endured

And lasted long enough to live the life we are meant
to

Run

The eastern wind and the western sun
Watched us move as we learned how to run
Gazing upon blown dandelions
Trying to reach the farthest horizon
Even the moon and the stars watched us at play
Trying to predict what will we be everyday
Just keep them guessing, pausing and pondering
Not letting them in on what is happening
Trying to be whimsical at a joker's jest
None can see how far we have become
Walking this life, trying to find our reality…

Melody

Hope is an unsung melody
When the heart is in despair
And the soul is made weary
By life's dreary air
Hope is the solace that opens your eyes
To little blessings and new beginnings
Each day, as you continue to thrive
Hope is that little voice inside you
Whispering words of encouragement
Deciding whether to head on or to tarry
It says, "Don't worry, I have got your back".

Memories

Welcome in sweet gratitude

All memories flowing from childhood

Those unforgettable naughtiness at a young age

Seemed to be clear and vivid as if watching a movie

Listening to litany of reminders to steer us away from wrong ways

To live life as true and honest as it can be

We all live in different circles and different realities

And it is kind of tough and hard growing up

I guess it was meant to be lived that way: to live our lives

Just as we have lived and gone through it

We are resilient now as we are ought to be

Because of those gone days

Shaped by our past, we lived this life with all those memories

That strengthen us and help us brave our present reveries.

"Hopes are born every second"
(*@chanticleer9*)

And just like what my friend @chanticleer9 wrote

Hopes are born every second

And it is true, I suppose

For however long the journey have been

How sad and tragically grieving our hearts have seen

We always pull through, but not with magic or any other taboo

But *we rise again with hope renewed*

That is shining its light on things anew

Hopes are born every second, I believe this now to be true

For how else could I be telling you this

After all the strife that I have been through

Poems by Ruth Jocutan

Fight and Flight

The ship is sinking, you tried to grasp his hand.

Holding aloft to his colorful words, slowly to disband.

In ambiguity you are left drowning—

Given up the last vest to him without knowing how to swim.

You heard a random call:

"Reach the shore! Please do try it!

Paddle your hands and kick-off your feet.

Try to float a little longer—

Fight for your life; on this ocean of troubles, do your flight"

-the voice resounded.

Until you found yourself exhausted lying on the ground.

You opened your eyes and smiled—

With a genuine and gentle heart.

You are safe and sound.

Surrounded by people who stretch-forth their hands.
They guide you home; to your solid ground.
They warmed your cold feet and hands,
Hugs and kisses they give as soon as you land.

Cradle of Hope

The cradle of hope continues to hide,
No matter how hard you tried to glide.
Clouded thoughts of betrayal sounds—
Clicking and clacking like wind chimes.

Enter your thoughts, creeping side by side.
Tormenting feeling you can never hide.
Catastrophic doom continues to bite.
When will you acknowledge that hindsight?

Cry for help, don't be shy—
There is a willing heart somehow,
It is ready to listen and understand,
You just need to stretch-out your hands.

Dreamt Reality

Within the abyss of darkness
You walk every corner and crests—
The levitating feeling of loss,
Seems like you are thrown and tossed.

The clamor of disbelief
Is a pedestal of grief?
With fervent accord you tried to grip—
Not letting any blood drip.

Dawning sunshine, a surreal feeling of glee.
Bringing hope and making you see.
That the becoming of your dreamt reality,
Is coming near to aid you purposely.

Sky Butterflies

Pounding head, sounding dread.

A catastrophe you continue to face.

Invisible prison you continue to dwell.

When will you break this unseen spell?

Magically, doubts will soon fly.

Maybe not as soon as the night draws nigh.

Or it will take another so-called eventide.

But, surely it will pass as the butterflies aim at the sky.

Wordsmith's Tale

Cluttering thoughts reeling inside your head.

Skimping moments you must live.

Dark swirl, leaving you in pirouette,

My heart; you want to put on a tourniquet.

The pain you learned to befriend with,

Within the posterior walls of your boudoir herewith,

Living a drastic life of a mere wordsmith—

 Keeping your words war with you forthwith.

With regular intervals you scythe those negativities.

Curving with a mighty heart your traits to be.

To handle such pain needs no hurry.

Just a will to be healed eventually!

Up Again

Aesthetic feels,

Aesthetic reels.

Trying to stand still,

Gazing on that window sill.

Familiar haunting debris of broken soul.

Finding your room, where to console.

The sun is up again,

Another day will begin.

Your Own Soldier

They said that *"change is inevitable."*

A phrase that somehow tells all is possible.

The ruins that you once lived on,

And the rubbles you have been ironed with and born.

To whom do you cry for help?

As you master your feelings, whelp.

To cry your deepest dismay,

Fitting standards the society keeps at bay.

Cheer up, hold your head high.

Carry on! You're not dead to lay.

Take heart, continue your battle.

No one is better; be your own soldier!

Cry

Do not cry because you are weak,
Do cry as a counterpart of being meek.
Divine help, you may continue to seek.
Hide your emotions not in a way so sleek.

Cry out your supplications and praise.
Let your worries be lifted up and raised.
Credentials do not weigh the credit.
Be the standard of your own merit.

Re-birth of a Firefly

The world is covered with darkness.

And the oblivion speaks for itself.

Everything is shattered and is in total mess.

Ideals are broken, the dreams you hold constantly change.

Wind howling from far-north,

Brings chills to you henceforth.

Where to seek that solitude?

Why do you need to hide from the multitude?

Close your eyes, fight your fears.

Look up from those flying within the horizon.

With their shimmering lights how beautiful they seem?

Fireflies do bring wonder and flame.

They lit up the pitch black firmament.

They may not illuminate the heavens,

But their glowing light does majestic wonders.
To fire your heart and live hope here after.
 Let the firefly in you burst its light,
Carry the torch you got from the start.
Bearing the light that sets you apart.
Re-birth in elusive wonders of art.

Pass in Haste

The moon shines not for every single night.

In every perigee and apogee there is varying distance.

Sometimes you don't see, sometimes too near to take a stance.

Collectively taking a phase to pause and to show its light.

Dark days do come to you,

Thinking that your moon lover abandoned you.

But looking at the stars with their fragmented lights.

Is a reminder that you are constantly guided in your nights.

The rain showers and thunderstorms do come.

Making you realize the comfort brought in the walls of home.

The feeling of sadness that glooms your every day.

They're worth experiencing to realize what happiness is at the end of day.

A melancholic dilemma you feel today.

And the constant reminders keep you worried.

With all the trouble and trials you face,

May they give you hope that in time—

They will pass in haste.

Poems by Angelita Dela Cruz

Self-Love

You once despised the moon and its light,

Whenever your sight reaches the sky in the night,

You can't help but to cry in silent and just hug yourself tight

Whispering a song to ease the pain yet asking to yourself,

"Why are you so plain?"

Sharp tongues of a judgmental society,

Their voices are louder than your sobs in the balcony.

You wear nothing but a plain and scarred body,

You believed that you never possess a face of a beauty.

The moon smiles at you,

Tells you that everything has its own beauty.

Your shape, your skin's color has nothing to do

Cause the real beauty is within you.

Your deep wounds that left you scarred,

You can cover it with love,

You can turn it as your own art

and beat the noise of your doubts.

A Burning Compassion To Someone

Hey dreamer,

I know life isn't that good lately,

life turns you into a mess you really don't want to be.

I do care a lot for you,

I understand that you want to have a deep rest

when the gloomy night surrounds you.

Hey, it's okay.

Even if the shadows living in those four corners of an empty room

scare you in stepping out of your comfort zone,

Even if the echo of the silence that breaks the noise in your mind

troubles you to have a peaceful rest at night,

Even if the sobs you hardly hide bring heaviness in your chest

that makes your soul can't move a single step.

Hey, all is well.

Just take some rest.

Nothing is wrong with you,

It's just a day that is a little bit unwell to you, I guess.

You can get through it,

I believe.

I believe in you.

Rest

You poured out love easily

like how the sky drops every bit of its tears to the ground of uncertainty.

Is it the heavy rainy season that bombs your peaceful night?

Where in your warm blanket you cuddled with the untold regrets,

You let the memories crawled again during your rest—

And here you are, again,

Losing the hope that you kept for your sanity.

Anxiety fills the mind when it is empty,

You better watch yourself when you are lonely.

You have lot of rooms in your head,

open only those chambers that will revive you from death.

Remember, my friend.

You can get up from that bed, put your hand out the
window,

Feel the cold touch of droplets, and ask for heaven's
help.

Pray.

Don't let the tiny voices steal your life,

or ruin the peacefulness in your mind.

There is grace during the season of darkness,

You can rest even in the midst of distress.

Waves of Hope

Like how waves travel with a purpose
along the sea and coming back to the shore,
you have a vision to see the real image of reality.

The people, our home,
our beloved country.
You have the light,
that is within that burning heart.
Compassion and love,
a vision that reflects hope
in every humankind.

Share that vision.
Let every sight see the real beauty
when they reach your hand.
Let them realize that there is still hope
after digesting the worst reality of life.

You've seen the world, the worsts were not a secret anymore

And a wave can make a difference in the wide sea or even in shore.

Let the truth of reality be the burden of your soul,

Let your wave sail and snatch the world

from drowning in the abyss of fools.

Why Am I Here?

Maybe you are asking this common question,
"Why am I here?"
Listed down every possible reason,
but you're just living like a dead person.

Why are you here?
Why do you exist in this sphere?
You walked without light,
You lived like a hungry wild parasite.

Craving for something in the dark
and want to be temporarily satisfied,
But you can't find life
and you can't see the triumph
in every step you had.

Listen.
Listen to the beating of that heart,
Listen and let me remind

that you,

a beautiful creation of God,

you are here to fulfill the mission He prophesized.

Faith

Hope

Love

Look from the above

and there you'll find,

the Maker of life,

who knew your desire to be found.

A Hopeful Piece for a Hopeless Poet

A broken road you might notice,

Like how life broke down your life during your pleas.

You can't deny the sorrow from within,

You hate life as if it was an enemy that is unseen.

You struggled from the very first start

and believed that

your whole life is a failure until the day you'll die,

It curved a scar in that heart

and burdens your genuine smile

every time.

I tell you, it was all a lie.

Who knows your future more than the one who gave life?

Who can see your destination until the day you will die?

I tell you, it was all a lie.

For the destiny isn't all about luck,
And your story was already written out of love.

A broken road it is
but there is a beautiful promise.
Life is dark in the process
but a light,
a spotlight
is where that will end.

You Are A Warrior

Maybe you've experienced a sudden loss of something important,

Maybe you've been in the ground of failure many times.

Maybe you've suffered from rejection every single attempt,

Maybe you've attempted to end your life multiple times.

You ended up being pessimistic about life

because of those trials and obstacle.

Life is a complete series of problems

and thus, you have to face every battle.

You have a warrior's heart.

You have a warrior's soul.

Soar above every pressure.

Uncertainty is real but rest assured,

You only have to believe that you are able to conquer

The dreams that are waiting of its rightful owner

Scars Into Hope

Scars were painted in your flawless skin, visible in your nakedness that lies all the evidences of those tragic scene. You were broken inside and out, your face was masked up with the bitterness you tried to hide.

Your heart was blinded

by pity and agony,

seems like you are dead.

You hid yourself from the world, isolated your dreams in your hand and you stopped to tell even in the mirror the appreciations you always wanted to hear back then. You let yourself bleed and not minding the crowd who tried to get an access to you.

You locked up your life,

let the darkness made you numb,

serenades your night.

You programmed your lips with the simplest answers you could respond for in that way you believed you wouldn't bother anyone with the chaos you were suffering. You took care of those scars by your own, you let them grow and normalized your soul. You have them, they were with you and they didn't depart every minute of your life.

A full acceptance,

Life of an independent.

You lived life alone.

You faced your battles alone but can't you see that someone wants to help you? You have me. You have your family. You have them whom you can rest your shoulder when times isn't that easy, you don't have to carry all the baggage in your own. You deserve a hand; you deserve a light in the midst of the dark.

Masterpiece in the World of Art

In a world full of artists;

poems and poetry,

arts and photography,

drama and music industry,

You, who is an art,

is the most precious among all of thee.

Even though you feel like your life is a void,

Miserable in every step, there is doubt

and even regrets you can't avoid,

Courage hid from your sight

and fear is all that left is in your heart,

An empty canvas you always see in the mirror,

A blank paper that no one wants to remember.

Insecurities you never talked about,

you've been keeping them all day and night.

The familiar feeling of emptiness sways you to fill
your mind

with the lies that you aren't really beautiful,

Leading you to hate yourself and dream of another
soul.

I know that's too hard to control,

too hard to overcome.

Staring blankly with your plain reflection,

Damages your hope and self-appreciation.

But you know what?

You are a wonderful foundation!

Still a masterpiece in a blank,

A great worth is in your hand.

No one can steal your identity and purpose

You are still an art,

Even if life is too harsh.

Colors of Life

Colors, light and dark,
Is it dull like how life started?
Or dazzling like the dreams you pronounced?
Living in this imperfect world of life and death,
Dangers and pests along the way;
wandering where is the end,
you've been lost and devastated.

Where are you?
Which color of life do you belong to?

Open your eyes and look around
Feel who is standing in that ground,
That's you, your soul that is found
And the person winning every battleground.

Stand and be blessed,
in your naked eye, all is lifeless
but behold,

battles you won are being counted—

Remember,

you are a work in progress.

About the Authors

Ashley Oting

A high school teacher by day, and a nocturnal animal with her face buried on her laptop, busy writing, by the time the night falls.

A huge fan of Taylor Swift and her music, a bookworm who adores Dorian Gray no matter how much of a red flag he is, and a lover of the classical arts and literature.

Someone who is still learning how to play the piano, her very first love, and someone who is in love with words and prose.

A bit introverted and a bit extroverted at the same time, and a woman whose favorite color is blue. People know her by her nickname on her socials as, Seya. But she is Ashley Oting, a woman with dreams that are yet to be reached.

Bon Ramniel Morales

Bon Ramniel "Bon/Niel" Morales, born on 21st of April 2005 is a writer from Lucena City, Province of Quezon. A student Journalist, Academic Achiever, Digital Artist and a Spoken Poetry Artist. His pen name nieletra_ is derived from his second name Ramniel and it is associated with the use of letters; "ni-letra" or made to by using the letter. He who writes in a native language that he loves. Pouring his heart and soul into his pieces, creating an art.

Jhannah Paguyo

Jhannah Rayzel D. Paguyo, who goes by the pen name unknownymouself_ on Instagram, is an aspiring writer from Taguig City, Philippines, living her twenty years with full of roller coaster ride. Life is indeed hard for her to go on. Before, she was a lost soul who was trying to find her lost pen. Her life was full of twist and turns but through writing, she found her refuge. She is not good at expressing her thoughts, but using her pen she can speak for herself and bleed her soul. Her masterpieces are all about grief, longing, and tragic love that might be too dark for someone but it is her way in expressing solace. She wants her readers to feel that they are not alone in those distressing moments and somehow they can find comfort in her poems. Writing to her is to mend the catastrophic pieces of one's heart. She believes that one can turn brokenness into art.

Judy Azul

Judy Azul is a budding writer hailing from Sorsogon, Philippines. She often writes structured poetry pieces that tackle various themes such as life experiences, love, hope, and society. To her, writing is like a catharsis- a means to express the words she cannot say. Her poems are usually written in English, Filipino, and Bicol Language. She is sharing some of her works on her Instagram account @sentido.1291 and facebook page named "Sentido" to reach more readers and fellow writers.

Jessa Erandio

Jessa Erandio or "Jez" is a writer from the Philippines. In 2021, she started her Instagram page called "Between Lines and Verses" to focus more on writing opportunities. This year, she has published her debut book entitled Your Universe and co-authored different anthologies published globally. She is an underwriter by profession and a writer by passion. She does social works through outreach programs and community services. She also plays different musical instruments which she uses primarily to compose songs.

Danna Garbida

Danna Espocia Garbida is known as dainspirights_ on IG and Facebook. She is an aspiring poet who lives in the county side of Sorsogon, Philippines. She has been reading a lot of poetry, thus she calls herself an aesthete - someone who loves reading poetry. She writes life poetry and some motivational poems in Tagalog, and English and likes to share some rare words to inspire. She only started writing poetry in her journal/diary. She wasn't supposed to be a poet and writer, it is only loneliness that made her poetry alive. She is part of the LGBTQ+ community, thus, she shines like a rainbow in the morning and like a candle at night. She finds it hard to write all her pieces and she doubts if she deserves to be happy. Yet, as you read her poetry, every line was chased by the pain she killed.

Angelo Estudillo

Angelo is a promising writer. One day, he hopes to publish his own book. Books that are intended to encourage readers and share the author's life experiences. Currently, he deepens his love of writing by· including narratives in his photography or by creating aesthetic visuals for the stories he has in mind. He enjoys reading, taking pictures, and the outdoors. His Instagram account "casual_ narratives" allows you to view some of his compositions.

Noemi Bucasas

She is from the Philippines and goes by the IG handle @imeon43.

Trying to raise towering teenagers with extremely opposite moods and behaviors is a challenge to her, not to mention working full time to support their needs, so she turns to writing poetry as a means of escape and to lessen the stress of everyday life. Most of her poems are basically what she feels and what she thinks at the moment; She has written for other poet's prompts which is a great exercise to practice the mind. This form of social media has helped her expand her interaction and views as she reads and internalizes other poets' works.

Jerraine Ruth Jocutan

Jerraine Ruth D. Jocutan's foundation for writing began at an early age. She used to attend writing workshops and trainings which developed not just her skill in writing but a profound love to hone her craft. Her journaling of her daily life paved the way for her to practice her writing skills. She recently published her debut book titled "An Access To My Heart (My Tell All)"; a compilation of poetry pieces inspired by her journal entries for the last ten years. She is a frustrated novelist turned poet. She goes by the handle name @walangtinta in Instagram, where she randomly shares her poetry as she labels herself as *"another random writer".*

Angelita Dela Cruz

Angelita Martinez Dela Cruz is from the northern part of the Philippines. She is a college student residing at Cagayan Valley, a proud Ilocano writer from the north who passionately writes poems about life and love. She loves poetry and her passion in writing fueled more when she met a family of writers on Instagram that helped her to bleed more rhymes. She already wrote a hundred poetry pieces that were uploaded in her poetry accounts on Instagram. She uses her ability in rhymes to make pieces that are timely, but most of the time, her writings are all about her life, her experiences in her personal battles. She's committed to reaching and helping people through her poetry. And she's dreaming of having her own published poetry book someday. She is the bleeding poetess behind the poetry account named *@eyngelwrites*.

There is a fire of hope within.
A COLLABORATIVE PROJECT
OF PROSE AND POEMS ABOUT HOPE

* 9 7 8 9 3 6 0 1 6 3 3 2 7 *